REACHING FOR THE STARS

A MISSION TO SPACE

WRITTEN BY ROXANNE TROUP
ILLUSTRATED BY AMANDA LENZ

Schiffer Kids
4880 Lower Valley Road, Atglen, PA 19310

For years, NASA planned an exciting new mission.
Just a few more minutes until ignition.

On this **lunar** adventure,
our four-person crew

will assemble

and test . . .

and scout the moon too.

The crowds have all gathered.
The cameras are rolling.

My family is here to watch the unfolding.

(Though strapped in together is a bit of a squeeze.)

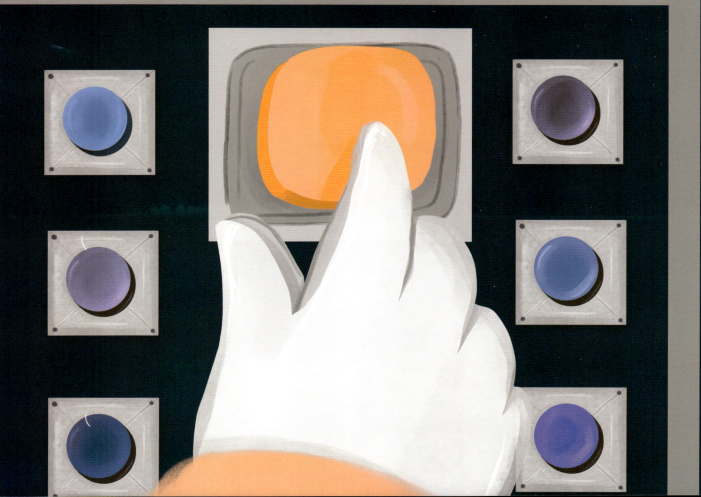

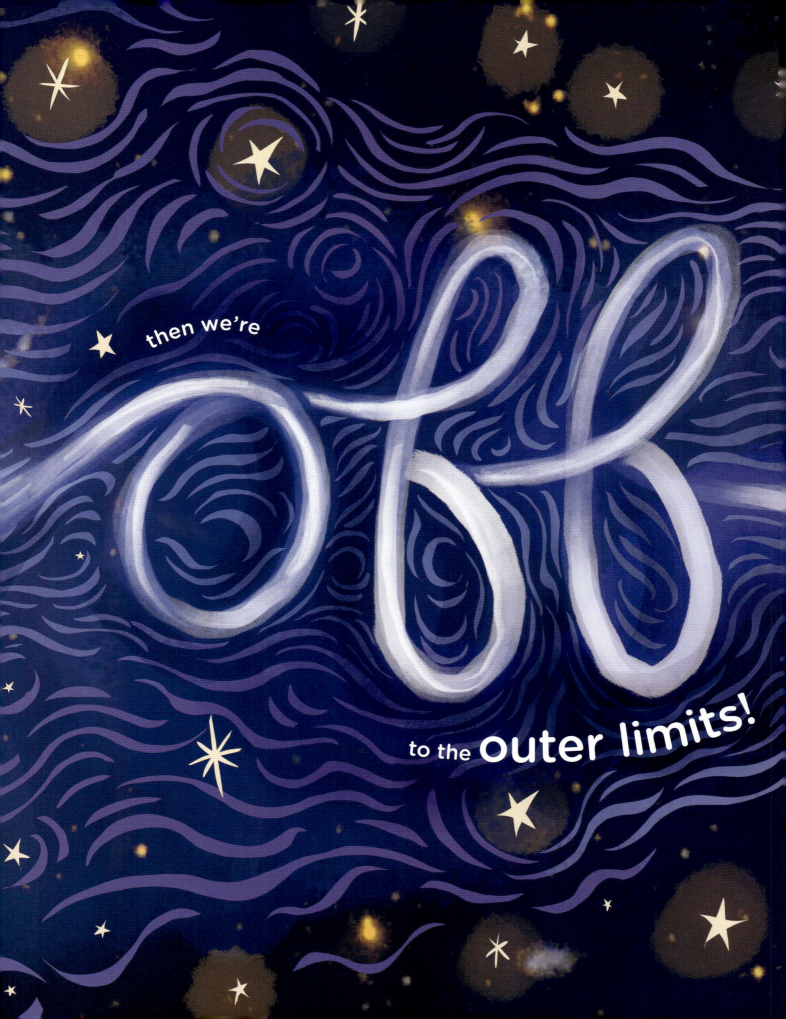

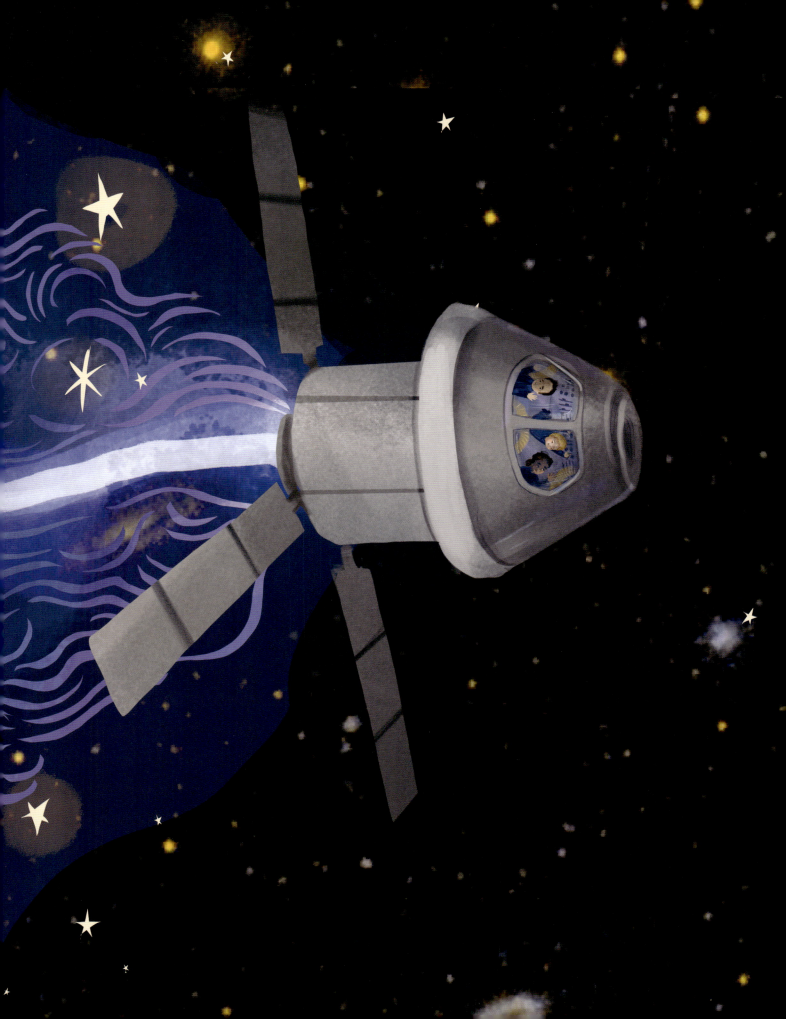

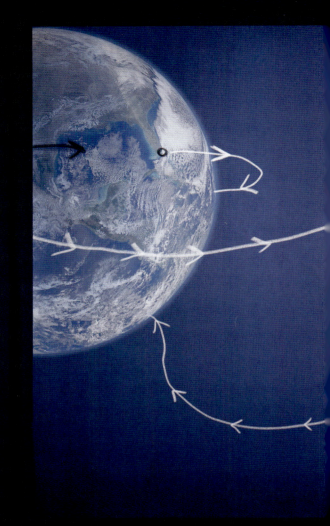
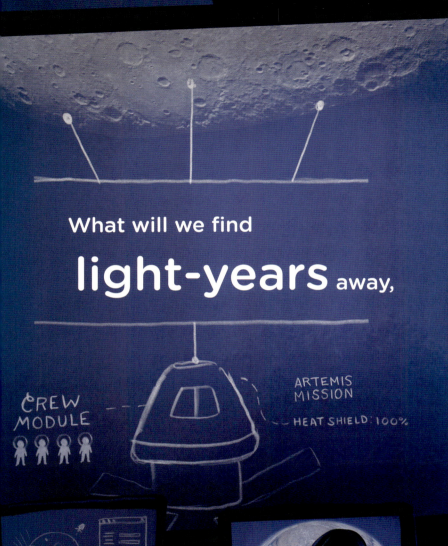

What will we find **light-years** away,

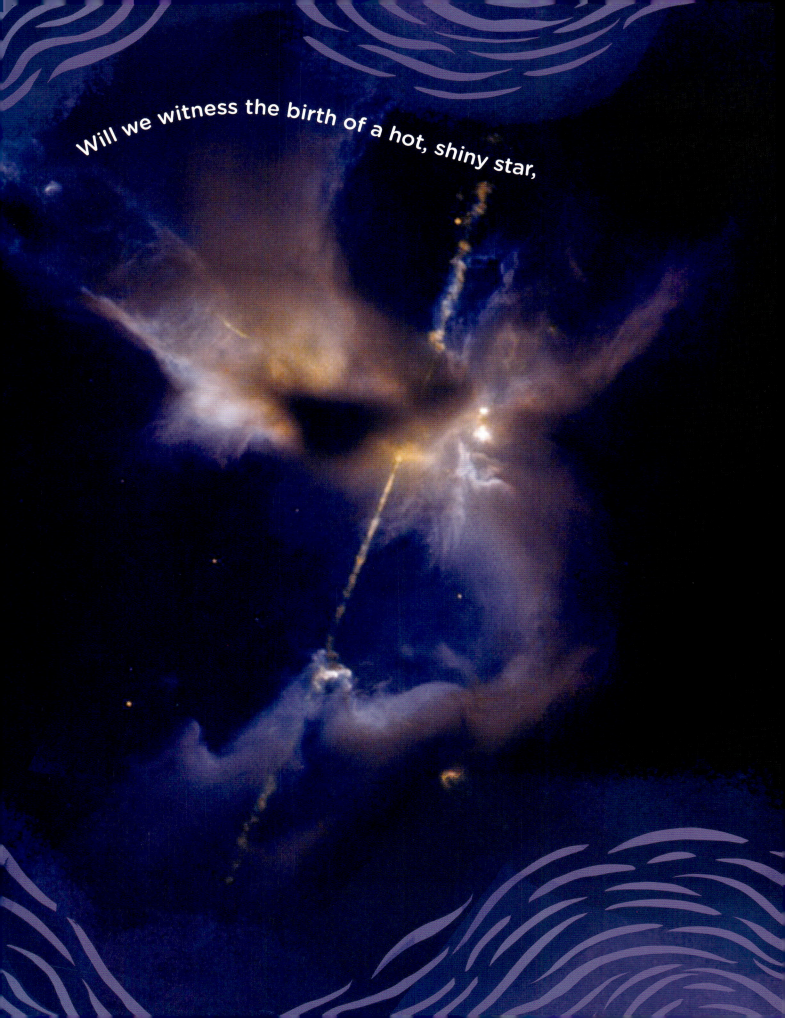

Will we witness the birth of a hot, shiny star,

or spy icy **comets** zip by from afar?

...or a galaxy shaped like a wacky balloon.

I'll trace every star of Ursa the Bear,

then scout the sky for Lepus the Hare.

It's easy to spot Leo the Lion.

He's chasing two dogs

and the hunter, Orion.

to observe,

and to learn.

As we blast into the great unknown,

could we stumble upon a
Goldilocks zone?

We skim through the void.
Who knows what we'll find?

The cosmos before us—the world behind.

WORDS THAT ARE

LIGHT-YEAR: 5.8 trillion miles, or the distance light travels in one year. Scientists measure the large distances in space by using light-years.

PLANET: A large, spherical body that orbits a star. Earth is one of eight planets in our solar system.

COMET: A bright, cosmic ball of ice, dust, and rock that orbits the sun. Comets speed up as they near the sun. There, a comet's ice begins to melt into a gaseous tail. The Greeks called comets "long-haired stars."

METEOR: A falling space rock that burns up in a planet's atmosphere, forming a streak of light. Before falling, meteors are called meteoroids. When seen from Earth, meteors look like falling stars.

NEBULA: A bright space cloud of gas and dust. Nebulae form in the space between stars and sometimes give birth to new stars.

CONSTELLATION: A group of stars that appear to form shapes. Ancient cultures used constellations such as Orion and Ursa Major (the Great Bear) to navigate.

OUT OF THIS WORLD!

LUNAR: Related to the moon. As the moon orbits Earth, it appears to reflect differing amounts of light. We call these variations lunar phases.

"Gs": Gravitational force. When accelerating into space, astronauts feel three or more times the normal force of gravity, which on Earth is 1G.

GOLDILOCKS ZONE: The "not too hot, not too cold, just right" distance from a star where water may exist on a planet's surface.

"T": NASA's countdown to launch. Each milestone within the countdown initiates certain tasks and procedures needed for a safe rocket launch (the "T" stands for "test"). NASA begins their "T-minus" countdown 43 hours before liftoff.

COSMOS: The universe. Our universe is a huge, complex system that keeps expanding. At present, it holds an estimated 200 billion galaxies filled with hundreds of millions of stars each. Talk about a cosmic astronaut playground!

AUTHOR'S NOTE

In early 2019, NASA announced a new program, aptly named Artemis, to celebrate the 50-year anniversary of landing on the moon. In Greek mythology, Artemis is the twin sister of Apollo (the name of NASA's first moon program) and the goddess of the moon. Working with countries around the globe, this new program was launched to return astronauts to the moon.

Since 1961, approximately 600 people have been to outer space. As of March 2023, only 72 of those space travelers were women, but no woman has ever been to the moon. Artemis was created to change that. NASA's announcement committed to landing "the first woman and first person of color" on the moon and using the knowledge gleaned from that trip to take humanity's "next giant leap"—to Mars.

You can learn more about the Artemis program on NASA's website: www.nasa.gov/humans-in-space/artemis/.

ILLUSTRATOR'S NOTE

The artwork within the book was created using NASA photos seamlessly collaged with illustration. Planet surfaces, stars, and comets are just a few of the images collaged with the digital illustrations. Can you spot all the images of the cosmos within the book?

(Hint: There's at least one on nearly every page.)

MORE SCHIFFER KIDS BOOKS ABOUT SPACE:

★ *I'm Going to Outer Space!*, Timothy Young, 978-0-7643-5385-7, $16.99

★ *Geraldine and the Space Bees*, Sol Regwan, 978-0-7643-5994-1, $16.99

★ *The 50 State Unofficial Meteorites: A Guidebook for Aspiring Meteoriticists*, Yinan Wang, 978-0-7643-6508-9, $18.99

★ *Escape Game Adventure: Trapped in Space*, Mélanie Vives and Rémi Prieur and illustrated by El Gunto, 978-0-7643-6031-2, $9.99

Text Copyright © 2024 by Roxanne Troup
Illustration Copyright © 2024 by Amanda Lenz

Library of Congress Control Number: 2024931517

All rights reserved. No part of this work may be reproduced or used in any form or by any means—graphic, electronic, or mechanical, including photocopying or information storage and retrieval systems—without written permission from the publisher.

The scanning, uploading, and distribution of this book or any part thereof via the Internet or any other means without the permission of the publisher is illegal and punishable by law. Please purchase only authorized editions and do not participate in or encourage the electronic piracy of copyrighted materials.

"Schiffer Kids" and the Schiffer Kids logo are registered trademarks of Schiffer Publishing, Ltd. Amelia logo is a trademark of Schiffer Publishing, Ltd.

Photographic image collected from images.nasa.gov.
Type set in Fandango/Gotham Rounded

ISBN: 978-0-7643-6817-2
Printed in China

Published by Schiffer Kids
An imprint of Schiffer Publishing, Ltd.
4880 Lower Valley Road
Atglen, PA 19310
Phone: (610) 593-1777; Fax: (610) 593-2002
Email: info@schifferbooks.com
Web: www.schifferkids.com

For our complete selection of fine books on this and related subjects, please visit our website at www.schifferbooks.com. You may also write for a free catalog.

Schiffer Publishing's titles are available at special discounts for bulk purchases for sales promotions or premiums. Special editions, including personalized covers, corporate imprints, and excerpts, can be created in large quantities for special needs. For more information, contact the publisher.